Visi

I turned to lo seemed to glow, to radiate from within. My mind knew that he must be from God, for only could one sent from God shine like this man shone.

"Joseph," he said again, "son of David. Don't be afraid to take Mary as your wife."

I wanted to protest. She had broken the vow. She had disregarded the law of Moses. She had committed adultery. And what hurt the most, she had shown no remorse for her actions. She actually was smiling at me as I discovered her condition.

Also by Benjamin Potter

Something Special at Leonard's Inn

Just a Simple Carpenter

Carpenter

The Story of Joseph

* * * * *

by
Benjamin Potter

Loom & Wheel Publishing
Kildare, Texas

JUST A SIMPLE CARPENTER
Published by
Loom & Wheel Publishing
P.O. Box 1691
Kildare, Texas 75562

First Printing: January 2000

Author photo ©1999 by TrueLove Photography — Cleveland, Georgia

Cover Art by Jane Potter

This fictional story is based on the biblical account of Joseph and Mary. The events held within this story are the product of the author's imagination. Any resemblance to actual people is purely coincidental.

ISBN: 0-9677668-0-X
Library of Congress Catalog Card Number: 99-97617

Printed in the United States of America by:
Morris Publishing
3212 East Highway 30
Kearney, Nebraska 68847
1-800-650-7888

*This one is for Thomas Preston Potter
and Martha Jane Weaver Potter—
You taught me about the real love of parents.
Thanks Mom and Dad*

Acknowledgments

I would like to thank all those who have helped and been an encouragement to me. I would especially like to thank those first readers Tom and Jane Potter for their input and suggestions. Again I would like to thank librarian and friend Kay Stephens for her help in editing this into a readable mess.

I would also like to thank those friends and family who have encouraged me along the way in writing.

I thank Jesus who became the center of Joseph and Mary's existence with the announcement of an angel, and who became the center of my life when I was six years old in Cason, Texas.

Just a Simple Carpenter

One

It was one of the most wonderful days of my life. My father had informed me that the deal was made. I would indeed marry the beautiful young Mary. I was sure the match would be perfect. Her family was well thought of in the community. She had a quietness about her that told of self-control not known to many of the younger women of marrying age. But like most young men who had begun the search for just the right wife, I had focused mainly on the beautiful eyes that seemed to pick up the smile that graced her face with radiance.

Each year as I grew older, I thanked God and my father for having the foresight to arrange a marriage with Mary's father when I was but five years old. And this day was the day that all the plans and promises would be fulfilled. This was the marriage ceremony. We were to be officially betrothed—espoused— looking forward to the day only ten short months away when we would conduct the wedding feast.

1

As I looked at my young bride, I knew that there would never be another for me. And from the look in her eyes (which she was quick to avert from mine, as was the custom), I could tell that she was also pleased with the arrangement.

I had worked hard in the shop. Taken extra jobs. Worked long hours to complete projects early with the possibility of a bonus in mind to complete the dowry.

For an artisan like myself, Hezekiah was awfully proud of his daughters. Especially Mary. After all she was his third daughter. I believed my offer of two goats and the barter of a new feasting table from my shop was very generous to present for the hand of the young woman. She would no longer be his burden; according to our laws, she would become my responsibility at the moment that the betrothal ceremony was completed. Then we could take anywhere from six months to a year to plan the wedding feast.

The table I offered alone—once finished—would be worth three days' wages to the potter that Hezekiah was. I feigned outrage when he had countered with a demand for a donkey, seven goats, five bolts of silk, *and* the feasting table. Gladly would I have presented that and much more for the privilege of marrying his daughter.

Although she was the third daughter, all the beauty of Israel rested in those expressive eyes now stealing another glance in my direction. No woman in Hezekiah's family nor anywhere in Nazareth drew even the slightest comparison to my Mary. I should not say "my" Mary, for she did not belong to me then, or now. Perhaps I belong to her. Yes, even now, my heart cannot be wrested from her tender grasp.

So after bargaining the like of which you may not even see in the marketplace, Hezekiah and I agreed upon the price of two goats, three lambs, one spotless cloak of virgin wool, and the feasting table. Once the ornamentation of the table was completed, I would be able to claim my bride.

The betrothal ceremony made my heart soar. Our fathers brought us together in the presence of all our family and friends. It seemed that all of Nazareth had turned out for the occasion. I was building a fair business making furniture and cabinets for many of the people in town. And Mary was the most-loved of all her father's daughters. She was quiet and beautiful with eyes that smiled even in sadness and a smile that radiated from within. It seems, as I look back, that I should have been able to tell that she had a special touch of God even before we were espoused.

In the simple ceremony that was so well-attended we exchanged promises of commitment and fidelity. It was too early to pledge love, although we both felt that our hearts were reaching for one another. I placed on her finger the simple ring of promise. I had saved my extra pennies for two years to have the coins to purchase a most elegant, awe-inspiring ring. Many of my cousins ridiculed me for spending a month's wages on a wife that might turn out to be a source of bitterness for me. But I would have none of it. I would begin the relationship with the best, for I would not have a wife who went to the well complaining about the abuses of her husband.

Everything pointed to the perfect life together. This is why I couldn't believe the report my friend Hoshea brought to me from his wife only three months after the betrothal ceremony.

Two

Mary's cousin Elizabeth was old—she was old and her priest of a husband was older still. Yet, they were going to have a baby. Oh, yes, we all knew the stories of Abram and Sarai. We knew that the Almighty could work wonders, and it seemed that He was creating one of the age-old blessings for this old-age couple.

Old Zechariah was not only too old to father children, but he had also remained silent from almost the time news came that Elizabeth would have a child. He had been performing the temple duties because his division had drawn the lot this particular year. I would have thought the idea of the blessing of a child coming to a couple so long without children should make the old priest shout for joy, but he either could not or would not talk!

You can imagine the gossip that all of this spawned. Not only did he not utter any words, but he also ran around gesturing like a madman. It was almost as if the Lord had struck him speechless. If it had been me in Zechariah's place, I don't think I could have held my peace. Word of this peculiar behavior arrived in the same messages bearing the glad tidings of the upcoming birth of a baby to the old couple.

Mary received the message from Elizabeth with a little trepidation. It seemed that my wife had begun to keep secrets to herself and the letter from Elizabeth disturbed her even more.

"Joseph, I must go to be with my cousin for a time. Having a baby is difficult even in the best of circumstances, and Elizabeth is well beyond the age of easily giving birth," Mary had told me. I knew that she was not only good with children, but that she could also help in the time of need when Elizabeth's baby would be born. Zechariah was no help at all. He ran around Jerusalem with his mouth bobbing open and shut like a fish out of water, with his arms flapping like a young eaglet testing its wings.

I wanted to protest, "What about our wedding?" I wanted to forbid her to go. She would have stayed had I said so. After all, I was her husband, even if we were still in the time of betrothal. And it was possible for her to be delayed in returning until after the appointed day of the official wedding. This was not a way to begin a life together.

As much as I hated to see my young bride go on

such a journey alone, I knew she was right. I could not go with her on this trip for I had still to finish the etching work on the wedding table if I was to finish it in time. Besides there was no one to travel with us as chaperon, a detail we could not ignore and keep the tongue-waggers at bay. Any appearance of impropriety this close to the wedding date would cast a dark cloud over the whole marriage. I did not concern myself with such matters—men would call on me to build their houses, furniture, and cabinets for them in any case . . . as long as my work remained quality. Mary—my beloved flower— should never be subjected to the sidelong glances and whispered innuendos offered by the careless people who lived around us.

So we decided that Mary should journey to Jerusalem alone to be with her cousin Elizabeth until the time came for her child to be born. She would travel on the main road by daylight only and remain until she saw that Elizabeth was out of danger. This job normally went to the mother of the woman giving birth, but Elizabeth's mother was three years dead by this time. Mary was the closest female relative capable of helping her cousin through the hard times of giving birth.

On the morning of her departure, Mary assured me that all would be fine. "The Lord goes with me," she said. "He is in control of even what is happening in our lives today."

"I know, Mary. I know," I said. "It is just so hard to see you go without being sure when I will see you again. Send a message with any news—and may it all be good news."

"Yes, my Joseph," Mary replied. "I will count the seconds until our wedding night." And she left. I felt that she wanted to tell me more but did not know how. So she left that way, walking up to Jerusalem without a backward glance. My heart felt the pain of the days without seeing her face, without hearing her voice, without knowing that she was only a stone's throw away.

Mary had been gone almost a month when Hoshea brought tidings from a trading trip to Jerusalem. "Joseph, my good friend!"

I smiled and embraced my old friend, "How was your trip, Hoshea? Were there many new fabrics for sale at the Jerusalem market? Did you happen to see Zechariah while you were there?"

"Slow down, my friend," Hoshea chuckled. There was a smile on his face but not in his eyes. "You are like a child who has discovered sweetbreads cooling unattended in his mother's kitchen. There is news from Jerusalem." Hoshea's face became a mask of concern. "Not all of it is good news, I'm afraid."

Hoshea proceeded to tell all that he learned from his cousin Rajeesh in Jerusalem. "Zechariah is continuing to perform his duties in the Temple even though he cannot speak. The elders are convinced that he has had an encounter with God and it has rendered him speechless. To conserve their precious paper for the preservation of the Scriptures, and for the mountains of letters they write to one another for no other reason than to make political contacts within the priesthood, they have not allowed Zechariah even the smallest scrap of paper—he must communicate with antics, gyrations, and gestures that make him look like a fool possessed of the Devil. They are sure though that his vision is not one brought on by sin or his life would have been destroyed. Some of the more jealous types in the synagogue have been heard saying that the Lord took Zechariah's voice as a sign that he should be stripped of his priestly position, but the elders have indicated that his vision was one that was so astonishing that it may be months before he is able to express himself in words.

"His wife seems to be his only pride, though. His priestly duties seem to be a drudgery that he endures until he can return to his wife's side. Rajeesh says that when he went to deliver some cloth to the old couple's house Zechariah was gazing down upon the spectacle of his wife as if she were a brand new bride. He literally beamed with pleasure and pride. Rajeesh says that it will not be long until this miracle of a baby is born to make the old couple even more famous than they already are. Imagine, God granting a baby to such an old couple as this—and Zechariah, a raving lunatic!"

"Ah, but Hoshea," I replied, "surely you will remember that Zechariah and Elizabeth have lived a most upright life. Many are the people in Nazareth who have wondered why it has taken God so long to bless them with a child. And now they will not only have a child, but a miracle as well."

Hoshea nodded and allowed that I was probably right. Then I could resist no longer, "But what of my Mary, Hoshea? Did your cousin see her when he was so busy gawking at her cousin and her husband?"

"Well, Joseph my friend," Hoshea hesitated as he began to reply. His eyes were cast downward in reluctance.

"Come now," I demanded. "We have been friends too long for you to treat me with such mysterious words and ways." Then the truth dawned on me. "What has happened to Mary? Was she harmed on her way to Jerusalem? Tell me, Hoshea, is my Mary all right?"

"Calm yourself, Joseph," Hoshea almost screamed in my face. He had his strong hands on my shoulder and was shaking me to calm my hysteria. "Mary is not injured. But Rajeesh did say that he saw her." I began to relax, though I could tell that my heart was still beating rapidly from my fear. Slowly, Hoshea continued with his bitter news, "I have not yet been able to confirm or deny the reports, though I trust that Rajeesh believes what he thinks he saw. Perhaps the woman simply looked like Mary. You know Rajeesh had only met her once, at your betrothal." Again, I was growing impatient, but I knew that my friend was trying to buy time, trying to figure out how to tell me something he thought I would not want to hear, trying to find the right words. "Joseph, Rajeesh says that Mary looked to be with child. I thought you said that you and she were abiding by the betrothal rules—"

"LIAR!" I screamed. I could not hold the anger within me. It turned to a rage as the words continued to sink in. Hoshea tried to defend himself, but I would not let him speak. "Your cousin Rajeesh has always been a liar. He is jealous that I was the one who won Mary's heart as well as her hand in marriage. We have pledged ourselves to one another. Mary would never betray me in such a manner. Not with another man—and we have not been together. Your cousin is mistaken. He must be. There is not a more devout woman in the entire district, including her cousin Elizabeth. I will go to Jerusalem. I will prove your cousin for the liar he is. And then I will have him brought up on charges before the Sanhedrin— for the Scriptures say, 'You will not bear false witness against your neighbor.' And carrying on this rumor—this gossip—about my wife is the same as bringing the charge against me."

When I had spent my energy on my words, Hoshea responded, "Yes, go Joseph. Go and find out the truth. For your sake, and your family's I hope that you find Rajeesh to be mistaken. But do not be shocked. It is not the first time that a couple did not wait the allotted time between the betrothal and marriage feast. Or it is not the first time that a young wife imprudently betrayed her husband when she could be easily found out."

"Because you are my friend of many years, Hoshea, I will allow you to say those things now," I said through clenched teeth and a tightened jaw. "But know this, neither I nor Mary have broken our vows—with one another or any other." I felt my hand tighten around the hammer that hung from a belt around my waist. "I will go. And cursed be the man who speaks against me or my beloved."

Three

I finished the ornamentation on the feasting table late that day. The wedding feast need only to be planned. I went to bed but could not sleep. Hoshea's words continued to bombard my mind.

He had taunted me at first, "Joseph! You devil, you! And here we all thought you were so straight-laced."

"What are you going on about, Hoshea?" I said bewilderedly. And more than a bit angry, "Can you not see that I am in the midst of completing the gift for my bride that we may be formally wed?"

"Ah, my friend. Isn't it a bit late for those preparations now?" He scoffed, winking with a rakish grin spreading across his face. I looked up from my work with an angry frown which caught my oldest friend off guard. I knew what he was insinuating—that

Mary or I, or both of us, had broken our vows of faithfulness to the marriage to come. And he knew that I did not appreciate such joking. Were it just my own name he slandered, I would have passed it off as jealousy for his betrothal ceremony was still months away, and I was finishing the last touches on the gift that would bring to me the long awaited marriage feast. But the story he told—on hearsay evidence from an unreliable cousin, I should say—brought shame to my Mary. My beloved Mary.

"I thought that you just decided not to wait for the ancient, backward religious traditions," he had said. "From what Rajeesh says he has seen, your intended hasn't."

The words haunted me now. Hours later. *"Are you really sure your beloved Mary is who you think she is?"* Yes, I told myself. I would trust Mary. I did trust Mary. We had loved each other since we were children and did not understand love. She would not, she could not betray me. I remembered the look in her eyes as I gave her my ring of pledge. She could not be carrying a child. I would not accept the word of the scoundrel Rajeesh. The creator of this lie against my beloved, my betrothed, my wife, would pay dearly. I would bring him up on charges of slander before the Sanhedrin. He would find difficulty in getting customers for the budding tailoring business he was trying to start in Jerusalem. No, he would find it an impossibility. How dare he even suggest . . .

But the doubt was there. Hoshea had been so

convincing even to the point of questioning whether I had been the one to suggest breaking the betrothal vows early. I tossed and turned. What little sleep I could find was filled with horrible nightmares of Mary attacked on the road. Mary alone in the city with no one but her old cousin and the speechless priest to protect her. And as her cousin was at the point of giving birth which would weaken her even more.

Mary had left three months earlier to be with her cousin. The time had given me more opportunity to work on the feasting table. But it also gave me opportunity to miss my Mary. Perhaps she had forgotten her promise to me. Perhaps she had not meant the promise in the first place. It would not have been the first time a woman had deceived her betrothed.

I rose early. Unable to sleep, I packed a small satchel with food for the journey, told my aging mother that I was going to visit Mary and her cousin in Jerusalem to let them know that the preparations for the wedding feast were at hand, and took a traveling staff in hand.

The stars were still out as I began my journey to the Holy City, but I traveled as a man who walked in the noon of the day. I walked with a purpose, as if I had a pressing appointment with the chief priests, or with the proconsul in Jerusalem. I had to see Mary, to prove Hoshea's cousin was a liar, to hold my beloved in my arms again. I was a man on a mission. I would bring Mary back untouched to become my wife. And the Lord would have to have mercy on those who spread vicious rumors, for I would not.

* * *

There was a great crowd around Zechariah's house when I arrived in the late afternoon. I could hear the commotion but could only make out a few of the words. It sounded like the men were all shouting their names, or the names of someone.

"Laban, it must be Laban," came one voice breaking through the din.

"Jacob," shouted another.

"Isaac! We have been three generations without an Isaac in the family!" insisted yet another.

As I came nearer to the crowd and could make more out in the confusion, a murmur drifted through the throng. "What?" I questioned a nearby on-looker. "What has happened here?"

The man turned to me and said, "Someone insists that Elizabeth is calling the child John. Can you believe? There has never been a John in this family. At the very least, Zechariah should name him for himself. Who ever heard of the mother naming the . . ."

The rest of his words were lost on me as I made my way through the crowded courtyard. And then I saw him. Zechariah, with his prayer shawl around his shoulders as if he had just completed his evening prayers, had come to stand just outside the door of their house. He held a precious piece of papyrus in his hands. It was large enough to create a small scroll, and he seemed to be preparing to write on it. Surely, I thought, he is not going to write some teachings down now. His son was apparently just born, and an increasingly agitated crowd is vying for the privilege to name the miracle son of the ancient mute priest.

But he did. He wrote. The papyrus was now permanently marked with the quill he held in his right hand. I could tell that he was making large letters, the kind sign-makers would use to create a massive wooden ornament to advertise a rich man's business. It only took a moment and then he straightened from his writing position. Silence grasped the crowd and strangled the last insistent champion for the name Isachar into a silence borne of curiosity.

Zechariah held up the parchment for all to see the signpost he had created. In letters so large that even the oldest man in the back of the courtyard could read it, the sign said,

"HIS NAME IS JOHN"

"No!" came the cries of the bewildered crowd. Some began screaming their more appropriate family choices again.

And then it happened. A strong voice rose above the noise, "SILENCE!" The air shook with the authority as all eyes turned again to Zechariah. "I am his father!" the old priest shouted with more strength than most men who had not been without a voice for the better part of a year. "The Lord God has named my son, and his name shall be John! Who among you dares to argue with the wisdom of the God of Abraham, and of Isaac, and of Jacob?"

Simply the sound of a voice coming from the man who had been unable to speak for so long caused a silence to fall upon the mob of kinsmen in the courtyard. Slowly, I watched them shuffle one by one to shake the hand of the old father and congratulate him on the birth of his son, John. At the end of eight days the newborn would be dedicated and formally named. But no one would question the naming again. He would be unique among the family of the old priest, for he bore a name unlike any of his ancestors.

* * *

I knew it would be some time before I would get to see Mary, for she would be helping Elizabeth through the time of purification required before the mother of a newborn baby could be a part of the family again. And since Mary undoubtedly had helped in the birthing process, she too would be required to participate in the rituals of purification before she could be a part of any public activity. I would have to wait eight days to see her. I would have to spend my time working to keep my mind off of the questions running through it.

Four

*****

I spent the next week working in the courtyard behind Zechariah's home. The old priest sat on a stool and recounted again and again the story of his son's miraculous birth.

"You would never believe it young man. I myself would not believe it had it not happened to me," he would say. "For years Elizabeth and I prayed that the Lord God would offer the blessing of a child. So long had we prayed that I had even told the Lord that a daughter would be all right. But it always seemed that He turned a deaf ear on me.

"Some of my brothers told me to give up. I should stop living an openly righteous life because it was plain to see that in private I had a deep-seated sin which kept me from fathering children. I, however, inclined my ear more readily to those who blamed

Elizabeth's barrenness on some hidden sin harbored in
her own heart. I knew that I lived according to the Law
and the Prophets. I assumed my wife did as well, but
one cannot see the heart—and she had not given me a
son, she had not borne me a child.

"Then the Lord God visited me. No, not the
Almighty Himself, but His messenger came and brought
us hope. 'You will have a son,' he had said. I laughed,
my boy. What a ludicrous idea! Me, an old man. My
wife, well beyond the age of giving birth. How could
we have children at our age?"

The old man told again how the angel struck him
with a mute tongue until after the child came, until after
his name had been settled on. John, a simple name for
such a miraculous child.

I had decided to make a cradle worthy of the
miracle baby the moment Zechariah found his voice
again. Miracle that this was, I almost longed for the
silence of a muted priest. I wanted a little quiet while I
worked, peace to think about all of this. I understood the
frustration of the old man who had been talked down to,
had been talked about because of his lack of children. I
had felt this same aggravation of late, friends
whispering about what they thought we did when no
one could see. Zechariah assured me that throughout
their childless years he and Elizabeth had been
completely righteous. Yet the people accused.

I knew that I had been faithful to the Scriptures
and to the traditions of a young husband who had not
yet seen his wedding feast. But rumors ran rampant

around Nazareth. People accused. First they accused me of not waiting to have relations with my bride. When they saw that I seriously had been faithful to our holy vows, they accused of worse. "Mary," they would say, "must have been unfaithful, then, to you, because . . ."

I almost marred the intricate design of the cradle I fashioned in my hands. The thought that perhaps Mary had been faithless tore at my heart. I asked again, as I had all week, "And you say that Mary, my wife, is doing well?"

"My son, you are most fortunate among men," he replied. "Your Mary is most radiant among women. Count the blessings of the Lord God."

And he would say no more.

* * *

On the seventh day I completed the cradle. It would be ready to receive the child the next day, the day of his consecration—his dedication to God. I looked forward to the ceremony. Zechariah made a special point to invite me. He said that he had no other way to repay me for the exquisite bed I had fashioned for his miracle son. I gladly accepted the invitation for it allowed me to be one of the first to see the baby, his mother, and her attendant—Mary.

After the priests finished with the ritual of circumcision and dedication to God in the custom of Israel I quickly scanned the faces behind the men. I could hardly believe my eyes when I saw her face.

Zechariah had spoken the truth. Not only was Mary
most radiant among women, not only did her face glow
with the beaming smile I remembered, but as I saw her
eyes, those eyes that smile into my heart, I could see that
she was even more beautiful than my feeble mind could
remember.

And then the crowd moved. Then I saw Mary. I
saw her fully. And my world crashed in around me.
Truth caved in from her obvious condition. Questions of
her fidelity no longer nagged at my mind. One question
replaced them all, "Why?"

Why had that scoundrel Rajeesh, that poor excuse
for a man, been right?

Why had Mary betrayed me? She could not hide
the fact that her time to deliver the baby drew near.

Why? Oh, why had I not seen it before? I had
loved the young woman before me. This woman who
now was obviously bearing a child. I had thought that
she loved me as well. I wanted to be angry, but I still
loved her. I turned and walked away. I must pray; I
must decide what to do. My wife, my very life, had
betrayed me. She had betrayed our vows. She had
betrayed God.

I could not stay in the house of Zechariah that
night. He had known. He must have known. But instead
of telling me, instead of warning me, he said, "She is
the most radiant of women. Count the blessings of the
Lord God." And then he returned to the tale of the
angelic visit announcing the birth of John.

I left Jerusalem and slept on the side of the road that night. Tears filled my eyes as I laid down. I had made my decision. I could not bear to keep Mary as my wife; she had been unfaithful. No one even mentioned that she had been attacked on the road to Jerusalem. She even seemed to be happy to be having a baby—a baby that I knew was not my own. No, she could not remain my wife. She had defiled herself before man and before God.

Neither could I hurt her. Yes, she was no longer the pure woman I had known at our betrothal just months before. But still my heart ached with love for her, a love I knew could never die. I had decided. I would divorce her. But I would do it quietly. I would find a way to keep her from having the disgrace of her unfaithfulness heaped upon her by a noisy public divorce. I would quietly go to her father. We would work out some way to keep Mary's sin from being further broadcast by the likes of Rajeesh and even my friend Hoshea. It could be done. And I would make it my last act of love for her.

I wept bitterly as I made my final decision. The only solution that satisfied my dilemma also bored deeply into my heart of love for Mary. Sleep born only of exhaustion overtook me, and I dreamed. I dreamed a dream like none I had ever dreamt before. Nor have I ever dreamt a dream like it since. I dreamt an angel.

Five

✳✳✳✳✳

J oseph, son of David," the voice came to me clearer than the voice of a friend seated across a table.

I turned to look for the voice and saw him. He seemed to glow, to radiate from within. My mind knew that he must be from God, for only could one sent from God shine like this man shone.

"Joseph," he said again, "son of David. Don't be afraid to take Mary as your wife."

I wanted to protest. She had broken the vow. She had disregarded the law of Moses. She had committed adultery. And what hurt the most, she had shown no remorse for her actions. She actually was smiling at me as I discovered her condition.

As I said, I wanted to protest, but for some reason I could not find my tongue. Perhaps my despair at my situation kept me from speaking. Perhaps my great fatigue overwhelmed me even as I dreamed. Perhaps the spectacle of the messenger sent from God to invade this dream took my words away. Try as I might to argue the point of righteousness, I could not. I wanted to say that because of my love for Mary, I planned to make the divorce as quiet as was possible; that although Mary had betrayed my trust, I would still treat her with a merciful hand, but the angel continued before the words formed on my lips.

"What is within her is the work of the Lord God Almighty," he said. "The child that she carries is from the Holy Spirit of the Living God. So do not be afraid to wed her. She will give birth to a son. You are to call him Jesus for he is one who will provide salvation for the sins of his people."

As the angel left me, a peace drifted into my spirit. I had been right all along. And even more importantly, Mary had been faithful. She had been more than faithful—God had chosen her for a special assignment. Mary's baby would bring salvation. I am just a simple carpenter, but I knew from my synagogue school that language such as this from God meant but one thing. God intended for Mary to give birth to the One, the Messiah, the Savior of all of Israel.

As selfish as it may seem, I realized that I too would enjoy the honor of this blessing. No father would have more pride than I in this son which would grace my home. Not even the miracle baby born to Zechariah and Elizabeth would hold a candle to this Jesus who would walk in my house, in my carpenter's shop, in my footsteps. What an honor! What a privilege! What a responsibility!

As I slept, my love for Mary grew. It multiplied. It compounded moment by moment. When I awoke early in the morning I could hardly wait to see my beloved.

I ran back to Jerusalem in the dawning hours. I beat with happy fists on the door of the old priest's house.

"Wha—" Zechariah did not look happy as he opened the door. "Joseph, be quiet. You will wake up the baby. He has just settled back after a restless night, and the women are asleep."

I ignored Zechariah. In my exuberance, I yelled for the house to hear, "Mary! Mary, come we must go home! The Lord has confirmed our wedding vows. We must celebrate!"

Mary rushed in from the back. She looked even more beautiful than I had ever seen her, the condition of motherhood growing in her womb, glowing on her face. She flew into my open arms, and we wept together the tears of joy and love. When I looked up, I saw Zechariah with his arm around his own wife who held their baby. They all smiled toward us—I believe the baby smiled, too. They knew. How they knew I did not know. But they knew what the angel had told me in the night.

I took Mary's hand and led her to the courtyard so that I could share with her my thoughts. We sat on a

low bench beside the garden and I told her. I told her of
the report of my friend Hoshea, which he had received
from his cousin Rajeesh. I told her of my desire to prove
them wrong, and of my heartache at the discovery that
she indeed had a child growing within her. I told her of
my plan to secretly divorce her so that she would see no
more disgrace. I poured out my heart's cry to her that
even when I thought she had betrayed me I could not
bear to hurt her. She held my hand and listened intently
as I awkwardly expressed my story. She occasionally
would insert, "Oh, Joseph," or "my poor dear, I am so
sorry."

"But Mary, that is not all," I hastened to add. And
then I told her of my dream, of the angel, the messenger
of God who had assured me of her faithfulness. I told
her how I knew that she had been chosen of God to
bring the Messiah into this world, how we had been
chosen to care for the baby Jesus until he grew to the
age when he could fulfill his calling. I noticed the shine
return to her face, the warmth of love return to her eyes,
as she realized that we would embark on this journey
together and that I knew without any doubt God's plan
was at work in my life, in her life, in our future
together.

"Oh, my Joseph. I could not tell you before," she
said when I had spent all the words that would come to
me. "But I, too have been visited by God's messenger."
Her excitement grew more as she shared with me her
encounter with the angel Gabriel.

* * *

"It was just before I left to come to Jerusalem. And Joseph, he came to me in the middle of the day! I was frightened at first, but then a warmth covered me, a warmth that I cannot describe. Then the angel said, 'Blessings on you, most favored among women! The Lord is with you.'

"He told me not to be afraid, that God had chosen me for a special task, that I would give birth to a son. I didn't know what to think. How could I, a virgin, give birth to a child? Joseph, I needed you there with me. How could I question the word of the Almighty God? But how could I betray my vow to remain faithful to you?

"'Do not fear,' he told me, 'for the child you will bear will be the Son of the Most High God. The Lord God will give him the throne of his father David, and he will reign over the house of Jacob forever. His kingdom will not end.'

"I then asked the messenger if he was sure of the message, 'How can I have a child when I have never been with a man?'

"'The Holy Spirit will come over you, and the Most High God will indwell you with His power, and you shall bring forth a son—a son who will be called the Son of God.' Then, Joseph, he told me of Elizabeth, of how she would have a child as well. And we both have seen that this is true. My barren cousin Elizabeth gave birth to a son, even in her old age.

"I could no longer question the word of God to me, Joseph. I said, 'I am the servant of the Lord. May it be with me as you have said.' And then he left me.

"I still wasn't sure whether to believe what the angel had said. I thought perhaps the day's heat had frustrated my mind. But when the angel's words concerning my cousin were true, I knew his message was from God."

Six

Mary and I stayed in Jerusalem to help out around Zechariah's home until the time was ended for Elizabeth's purification. So for another month Mary helped to keep the house clean, the meals prepared, and the baby entertained. I must admit that I was more than happy to play with little John, the miracle child. He smiled; he cooed; and he screamed for food, for sleep, and for clean clothes.

Playing with the baby made me begin to look forward to the time—now only a few months away— when Mary and I would have our own child to look after. I say our own child, but I knew then as I know now that I would only be the earthly protector of God's chosen One, a job I now most readily accepted.

Zechariah arranged for many of his friends to bring me small repair jobs so that I could earn my keep during our stay with them. When the month had passed, several of these customers begged me to move my business to Jerusalem. But I had too many well-cultivated clients at home in Nazareth to completely pull up stakes and move. Mary and I must return to our home and our families. We would tell them that God had led us to complete our wedding vows while we were in Jerusalem. Some would be disappointed that we had not returned to Nazareth for the feast, but all would congratulate us on our growing home. Hoshea would know, but he would say nothing because he understood my love for Mary and would accept my decision as an expression of that love.

We returned to greater hustle and bustle than our sleepy town normally saw even at feast times. Nazareth had not traditionally seen excitement and tourist swelling. But everywhere I turned as we entered the streets I saw people acting as if something were about to happen. I stopped a man on the street. "Excuse me," I said. "What is all of the furor about?"

"Everyone is preparing," he replied eyeing me as if I had just appeared from thin air.

"Preparing for what? I have been away for weeks, my friend," I said grabbing his arm to slow his progress.

"The taxing, young man, the taxing," he said. I could tell that he was beginning to get irritated with me, but I had to know.

"What taxing? Where and when shall I register?" I asked.

With a heavy sigh the man decided that he must tell this intolerable upstart everything, and so he explained, "In just three months everyone is to go to his ancestral home and register for the Augustin tax." The sarcasm in his voice dripped like a comb filled with bitter honey as he continued, "The *Great* Caesar has determined that he cannot live without more of our hard-earned denarii and so we must register. Many people are trying to sell some of their valuables so that they will not register so valuable. Others are planning to make a great family picnic and reunion out of the occasion. I am simply trying to get started on my journey. I must travel seven weeks to get to my destination. And I would like to arrive before most of the rabble. I hope to find decent lodging for the days of tax enrollment. If I were you, young man, I would take my pretty wife and beat the crowds to my ancestral home. As for me, I plan to sell what I have here and use the money to purchase a roadside inn. I will make a fortune." The man muttered to himself as he shifted his sight back onto his original destination.

So that was it. Caesar Augustus had declared a census to raise the tax rolls. I would have to travel again. Mary must go with me, for she was my wife. But Mary would not be able to walk all the way to Bethlehem. She had started to tire easily the last several miles of our journey home from Jerusalem. We had time; I would just wait to leave. Mary could rest while I made arrangements for us to go to the City of David, my most prominent ancestor.

Every day that we waited to leave Mary grew larger and more fragile. I knew that this trip would take much of her energy. I had to find a way for her to make the journey without walking every mile. I found a donkey for sale, but I am a simple carpenter and did not have the funds to purchase the beast. I knew that it would be an uncomfortable mode of travel for my wife and the baby growing within her, but I also knew that she would need the rest from walking as the day of delivery approached. I traded the only thing of value aside from my tools—the ornamented feasting table. For the table I received one donkey, an extra coat for Mary, and enough money to perhaps purchase lodging in Bethlehem for two nights.

I completed several jobs for merchants in Nazareth preparing for the registrants who would be traveling to our fair city. This work consisted mostly of door repairs and makeshift cot construction along with tables and chairs to add to the courtyards of the local inns. From this work I garnered enough money to purchase a light saddle for the animal and food for our journey. One month before the census, we began the journey to my town of ancestry, Bethlehem of Judah, the City of David.

We made awkwardly slow progress. Even without walking, Mary had to make frequent stops to rest from riding the jarring, bone-ridden donkey. So often did we have to stop that I began to question the wisdom of spending good money on such an evil animal. Tired of the flat bread and dried meat I had packed for the trip, I once threatened to butcher the beast on which my Mary rode to enjoy the taste of fresh meat. Once we stopped by a small spring of water—something told me I should make note of a spring in the desert—and Mary addressed my frustration with the quiet, loving determination that had stolen my heart even before we promised undying love in the betrothal ceremony.

"Oh, my!" she exclaimed. "Joseph, quickly!"

I rushed to her side. I had helped her to lean against a rock while she rested from riding the cantankerous old beast. I just knew something had gone awry with either her or the baby, the Son of the Most High. But when I reached her she guided my hands to touch her protruding stomach. "Oh, Joseph, he is kicking!" she whispered excitedly to me. "The baby is excited about travel—especially to the City of David. I know the time is near. The baby will be born in the village of the greatest king our people ever knew, save the Lord God himself." Tears of joy covered her cheeks as she added, "Joseph, the blessing of giving birth in Bethlehem. Think of it!"

Seven

Bethlehem had already begun to swell. I remembered the little village from visits to my uncle's house a time or two when I was a lad. What I remembered could never compare to the noise and press of the crowd that greeted us as we entered the edge of the town. We arrived just as the sun was dipping below the horizon, but we had no need of a torch or lantern. Merchants and innkeepers alike continued to light up the city streets, taking advantage of the carnival resulting from the enrolment decree.

Mary and I tried to stop at an inn just as we came into town, but the crowd at the door surged backward as two men burst from the entrance. "And some cousin you turned out to be, Reuben!" the older of the two men shouted over his shoulder.

A man with gray already peppering his beard

looked out of the now freed doorway and shouted back, "Had you been the first to meet my price, Eleazar, you would have had the last two pallets in my inn!" The man I assumed to be Reuben raised a craggy fist to the two men leaving the inn. Then he turned to the crowd and said, "And as for the rest of you, be on your way. There are no more beds to be had here."

Eleazar and his companion passed by grumbling to each other, "We are better off not staying in this high-priced dump. Reuben's linens are infested with fleas anyway. Perhaps there are other inns who still have space."

I looked at Mary. Her eyes were tired, but she smiled at me from her seat upon the donkey. I knew that she was weary from the traveling. I also knew that we must find a place to stay the night soon or the baby might come without a place to lay his head.

We approached our fourth inn of the evening almost ready to give up all hope and sleep under the stars yet one more time. "Wait here," I told Mary leaving her to rest by the beautiful small pool and fountain in the courtyard of the tiny inn. Turning to approach the door I saw a little man with very little hair emerge from the lamplit common room. The sign, freshly painted, hung from his hand. I saw that the sign said, "No Room."

He stopped me before I could turn to leave. His name was Leonard. How can I ever forget the kindness he showed to my little family that night. With every available inch of his hostel rented, he sent his servant to prepare a small corner of the stable at the back of the house. While he made these arrangements we met Sarah, his wife.

Sarah, as kindly as Leonard had welcomed us to stay, began welcoming us to leave, "We are just too packed tonight. Come back in a day or two, and maybe we will have a space. As for now, perhaps Lemuel down the street—"

We heard no more about Lemuel because Leonard shooed his wife away and led us to the stable where he and, yes, Sarah made us as comfortable as possible. Sarah did not express great happiness at our staying, but she acquiesced to her husband's wishes. I thought she might throw objects at both Leonard and me when he refused to accept the payment I offered for the lodging.

"How can I charge money for a barn stall?" he had said. And when Sarah opened her mouth to protest, Leonard raised a hand and said, "We cannot, my dear. Don't you see the condition of this young woman? Can you not recall how you tired so quickly? And maybe God will honor our home with the birth of a man-child."

They left us to try to get some sleep. Sleep eluded us greatly that night though. At first the noise of the household animals augmented by the stable-yard clamor of guests' animals (including our own wretched donkey) kept the sandman at bay. Then when it seemed the animals had quieted for the night the street racket which had accompanied the swelling population of the village disturbed our minds. Finally, when I felt it was safe to

lay my head on the straw pillow I had fashioned, Mary
began to cry out.

"Oh!"

"Mary, what is it?" I whispered hoarsely.

"Joseph, . . . I . . . think . . . it . . . is . . . time,"
she choked out through clenched teeth.

"Mary, oh, Mary. Now?" I said.

"Yes, NOW!" she screamed. "Go now . . . and
get, SARAH!" Her breath seemed to be coming in
short gasps now, and sweat formed on her brow.
"NOW, Joseph!" she managed to say, again between
clenched teeth.

Gathering my wits, I ran and summoned Leonard
and Sarah from their bed. I didn't have to be told twice.
Running back to the stable, Sarah began administering
aid to my wife as if she were a practiced midwife. In a
quiet moment between Mary's birth pains, Sarah
happened to look up and see Leonard and me standing
there like fish out of water.

"You, father," she said to me sharply. "Go and
make a bed of that manger. This baby will need some
place to sleep when he arrives." Turning to her husband
she scolded, "And you, the innkeeper who gives away
lodging bring me some soft cloths from our rooms. This
baby is ready to be born, and the men stand around like
trees blowing in the wind."

By the time I finished my task, I saw that
Leonard was back with the cloths. And then I heard the
noise. No longer was it the noise of barnyard or caravan
animals. No longer was it the cacophony of rowdy

travelers. But now it was the sweet song of fresh lungs singing unto God, "I am born. I am here. I am."

"Listen," Leonard said to me. "There is no more precious sound than the first cries of a newborn son." A tear came to the old innkeeper's eye. "Forgive me, Joseph," he said, "but I have longed for the moment when this house would hear just that sound. You see, twenty years ago Sarah and I were awaiting the birth of our first child. I knew without a doubt that God would grant my prayer for a son. And then," a shadow of bitterness and anger crept onto the brow of this man who had shown only kindness and mercy to Mary and me. "And then the thoughtless act of one I can no longer name brought about the destruction of my firstborn along with my happiness. Sarah was no longer able to have children after the shepherds drove a throng of excited sheep right into our courtyard as a joke. My wife was knocked off her feet, and while she survived the trampling, our son was stillborn within three days of the accident . . ."

His voice trailed off, and I felt his sorrow. It had settled deeply within his heart, had taken root there. It was this incident, I saw, that had magnified his compassion to me, a poor road-worn traveler leading a donkey that carried my young wife who was great with child. I could not have expected that God would use a twenty-year-old incident to keep His Son from being born out-of-doors. But then, I had not expected God to speak to both Mary and me through angels, ensuring the baby would have a family to provide for his needs as he grew.

After a moment the glint returned to Leonard's eye and he said, "But this is not a time to remember the sadness of so many years ago. It is a time to celebrate; let us look at the beautiful son your wife has given you."

Eight

We watched as Sarah helped Mary wrap the baby in the soft cloths Leonard had brought out from the house. Sarah doted like a grandmother; Mary smiled her quiet smile down on the baby; and Jesus moved from the loud screams of birth to the gentle cooing of contentment. Even the animals in the yard seemed to reverence the moment of birth for this special, angel-announced child.

I heard a sob in the quietness and turned to see a lone tear crawl down the innkeeper's face. His cheeks were wrinkled into the biggest smile I had yet seen on Leonard, who enjoyed a wide grin most of the time. "Thank you, Lord," I heard him whisper. "Thank you for letting me still be a part of something so important."

And then the stillness of the moment was blasted away by shouts and arguing from the street. Leonard and I ran to see what had happened and found about eight or ten rough-looking men ranging in age from young to old. The men were loud and almost obnoxious as they seemed to be searching the city. Their rabble was rousing the neighbors who stuck their heads out of doors and windows to call for quiet.

"You, shepherd," I heard one man call. "Go back to your sheep and leave us alone. Do you not know that it is still several hours before dawn? I must rest to be ready for a full day tomorrow."

"I just want to know if he is here," the oldest of the shepherds replied. "We are to find him in a manger, and there is only one left in town!"

"Jerome!" Leonard shouted. "Take your cohorts and your sheep and leave here. I thought I told you never to come here again. Besides you are too late this time. The baby is born; there are no families to ruin this time."

I knew in an instant that before me stood the shepherd Leonard held responsible for the loss of his son so many years ago. The face that had so recently wept gentle tears of joy at the birth of the miracle child now filled with rage and darkened slowly from the neck up.

Before Leonard could chase the shepherds away, Jerome pled his case, "We will leave, Leonard. But first we must know—this child you speak of, is he in the manger? Is he wrapped in strips of cloth?"

"As a matter of fact he is," Leonard replied cautiously. "And he is Joseph's son born only moments ago to the young mother Mary in my stable."

Jerome turned to his compatriots, some of whom were just arriving. "He is here!" the old shepherd cried. "We have found him! The angels' message is true!"

"What did you say?" I asked in disbelief.

"I said, 'The angels' message is true!" he repeated with more excitement than he had first used in his pronouncement.

"'The angel,' what angel?" I asked.

"Tonight," he explained, "we were visited by an angel who told us of the birth of the Chosen One in Bethlehem. He said we would find the baby wrapped in strips of cloth and lying in a manger. And then he was joined by a sky full of angels singing God's praise! We were so overwhelmed with this special message from God that we, all of us, left our flocks, all of them, to come and find the miracle child whose birth is announced by angels!"

I turned to Leonard who seemed to be losing some of his resolve to keep the shepherds out. "Leonard," I said, "we must let them come and see the baby, for this is no ordinary child. I was visited only a few weeks ago by an angel who told me wonders about the child that Mary carried the baby Jesus who now lies quietly in the generous gift of your manger and stable. Let them come."

I saw little of Leonard's reluctance left in his eyes. He understood that the peacefulness of the baby in the manger was not to be hoarded by one or two but should be shared with as many people as possible—even rugged shepherds.

As the two men who had been enemies because
of an accident years before gazed upon the Son of God,
I witnessed the icy fingers of anger and hateful feelings
melt away. Leonard put his hand on Jerome's shoulder
and the two watched as Jesus quietly wagged his hands
as if reaching out to them.

"I am sorry," a voice said behind me. I turned to
see another shepherd about the age of Leonard and
Jerome holding a lamb, a perfect lamb, in his arms.

"Joshua!" Jerome nearly shouted. "Where have
you been? You must see the baby the angels sang of."

"I am sorry," Joshua said again. "I could not
reclaim the foolishness of my youth. It was I, not
Jerome who destroyed your family and your child so
many years ago. Jerome wanted simply to provide the
best of the flock for the celebration of a boy-child's
birth. I thought we should make a joke and run the flock
through your courtyard first. Many is the night that I
have lost my sleep thinking about what happened to
your friendship because of my childish pranking.
Leonard, will you accept this, the finest of our flock, as
an offering to celebrate the birth of the new child?"

Leonard glanced at me, at Mary, and at Sarah.
We each nodded in turn, and the old innkeeper's face
radiated its ever-present grin, "We would not have it
any other way, Joshua. We must celebrate and thank
God for the gift to Joseph of a fine, healthy son!"

I knew what Leonard did not, the gift of this son
was a greater gift to me than any other God could give. I

would have the privilege, the responsibility of raising His Son!

Nine

Leonard helped me set up shop in Bethlehem while we waited on the completion of the census. I had sold most of my belongings to make the trip to Bethlehem. Coupled with the previous trip to Jerusalem the month before leaving for David's City I had depleted all of my resources. All I had left, in fact, included my tools which could not be sold and the stubborn donkey which must be sold. Not only did we need the money, but the animal served no practical purpose.

So we sold the donkey.

Leonard and Sarah were glad to move us into one of the empty rooms of the inn when the crowds started thinning out. In exchange, I repaired all of the broken furniture in the rooms. I also affected some repairs to the building itself, which had long since seen its last fresh coat of paint or new roofing. Leonard wasted no time in bringing in friends and neighbors to examine my work and augment my meager purse with more jobs than I could get to at once. One day I accused Leonard of forcing his neighbors to give me work so that we would stay on at the inn. I kept the buildings in good repair, and Leonard could play grandfather to Jesus.

The next afternoon Leonard returned from the market with news of a house for rent in the next street over. "If you would move out," he said, "I could rent the rooms for more than I would have to pay you to keep my inn in the best shape of all the hostels in town. And if you are just one street over, Mary can always bring the baby to visit with Sarah."

We gathered our belongings and moved the following morning.

By this time I had a steady stream of customers who came to me to repair their old furniture, to build them new furniture, or to patch up places in their houses. They all paid well, too. I must admit that my handiwork showed much more craft and skill than the other two carpenters in town ever achieved.

After we moved, Mary and I carried Jesus over to the inn almost daily on the pretext that he wanted to see "Grandpa Leonard" and "Grandma Sarah," but if we allowed ourselves to think about it, we adults enjoyed the company as much as the time playing with the baby. Often we found old Jerome seated at the table arguing over old times with Leonard. They carefully avoided the topic of the courtyard sheep stampede, and as the weeks turned into months, I could see the embers of the ancient friendship fanned into flame.

It was on one of these nights when Jesus was about twenty months old that Jerome had curious news. I walked in on the middle of the old friends' conversation.

"No, Leonard, I'm trying to tell you. Can you never listen," Jerome was saying. "It is a caravan."

"Yes, Jerome, so you said," the innkeeper countered. "And I said that we have caravans through here all the time. This is nothing spectacular."

"But it is spectacular, old fool," the shepherd returned. "This is no ordinary caravan. It is not from anywhere near here. One of the boys asked a servant where they had traveled from. And they said some name that no one could understand. He said they spoke with a very broken accent, unlike that of the Midianites or even the Samaritans."

"So these mysterious traders are from Egypt. What's so unusual about that?" Leonard said.

"Again you are not listening, Leonard," Jerome said, exasperated. Then he noticed that I had entered the common room of the inn. "Joseph, my *true* friend," he said to me, "tell me from which direction a caravan from Egypt would come."

"The west of course," I replied.

"Exactly! And this group travels from the *east* with elephants whose ears are so much smaller than any I have seen coming from Egypt," Jerome exclaimed. "And besides, Leonard old boy, this is no trade expedition. They are looking for a king. At least that's what the servant told Isaac."

We did not receive the visitors from the east for another three days.

* * *

They came into the yard where I had set up my workbench. I cannot describe the feeling that came over me when I looked upon the three leaders of the entourage. I use the word entourage because there is none other to describe the delegation standing before me now.

"Can you show us the Child King?" one of the men asked me. They were all three dressed like kings themselves.

"I don't understand," I replied. "There are no kings here. Only my son, my wife and I." I know, I know. Jesus was not really *my* son, but try to explain *that* to these strangers.

"He must be here," the man asserted. "Look!" He pointed to the sky, and I almost lost sight from the bright evening star that seemed to hover over our small house. "That is His star. We have traveled far—ever since the star appeared in the eastern sky. It is the star of a new king. Our charts confirm it." He swept his arm taking in the five servants carrying satchels bursting with scrolls.

"When did you say this star appeared?" I asked. When he told me the date, I knew that God had spoken in more than just the angels. The star appeared in their sky on the very night that Jesus was born. "Mary," I called, "come! And bring Jesus with you. We have very important visitors!"

The kings—they preferred the name Magi, wise ones—placed great store in their ceremony. They insisted that we sit in the shade as their servants rolled out a plush carpet and fanned us all with great palm branches. The focal point in this spectacle was Jesus. He sat between his mother and me, and I could have sworn he held his head up in the most regal of manners.

In a show of great pomp and circumstance, each of the three kings in turn presented Jesus with gifts fit only for a baby of royal birth. He received a casket of gold, a bottle of frankincense, and a vial of myrrh. I almost fainted at the sight.

Mary insisted that the kings remain with us. Leonard could not be jealous, because most of their party stayed in his humble inn. Jerome and Joshua even made some money from this throng because they hired out three of their shepherds to keep the livestock away from the sheep or the town.

The next morning as we prepared their breakfast, the spokesman of the Magi came to me with a look of urgency on his face.

"We are troubled, blessed young man," he said. "We had intended to return to your current king and bring him the location of the little one. He had said he wanted to come and worship him as well. But last night we dreamed—all of us—that Herod meant harm to and not worship for the baby king. We will return to our country another way. We will not put the baby in more danger."

What they said troubled me, too. And that night I dreamt again.

Ten

The Magi had left, and the day began to settle back to normal. That night my mind was troubled by another dream—another angel dream.

The angel came to me that night and said, "Joseph, do not fear. Take the child and his mother and get to Egypt."

"Is this related," I asked him, "to the dream the wise men had? Is Jesus in danger?"

"Pack quickly," he replied. "You must go down to Egypt and remain there until I tell you to return. Herod has plotted in his heart to try and kill the child."

I awoke with a start and called Mary. We packed hurriedly taking only as much as was necessary, only what we could carry. I fashioned a bag that would hang from my neck and could be loaded in both ends. Mary gathered her head shawl around her in such a manner that the child could ride in a small hammock formed at her side. Jesus did not wake as we stopped at the inn to roust Leonard and Sarah from their sleep.

I shared of the angel's warning and gave Leonard some of the gold from the Magi to purchase a donkey that we could pack our few necessities on and also use as transportation on our long journey into Egypt. Leonard kissed us all on the forehead, said, "Godspeed!" and turned away. I knew that he wanted to hide his tears from us.

Sarah made no such display. She wailed as if she had lost a child. I imagined that her mourning wail echoed the one she cried when her own son was delivered without life. Through the tears she bid us, "Go with God," kissed us, and watched from the door. In the midnight hour, as we left, I turned and saw the old couple turn back into the inn heaving great sobs of anguish and leaning on one another for more than just physical support.

I did not think about the scene that would play the next day when Jerome would show up to play with Jesus. The handmade wool doll that he would bring would never know its owner.

* * *

Years later I learned that we escaped Bethlehem at the precise moment needed to avoid the wrath of Herod. Unexpectedly, I ran into Isaac, Jerome's nephew and fellow shepherd, in Jerusalem. I asked about my old friend the innkeeper and learned of his deep loyalty to me, the child, and my family.

"Joseph, I am sorry. Both Leonard and Jerome are gone. Leonard died the day you left. Jerome left the flocks with Joshua, Josiah and me in order to help Sarah manage the inn. They married two years after Leonard's passing and Jerome died just last spring," he told me.

My heart sank in the depths of sadness as I listened to Isaac recount the events of the day that followed my midnight getaway.

"I went to town with Jerome to visit Leonard, see Jesus, and bring you another lamb to garnish your table with. Jerome said that the kings had left after having showered the child with gifts. Joshua said, 'We will not be outdone by rich foreigners bearing the trappings of gifts. We must show the carpenter and the mother of the angel night child who is really practical!' And together they chose the finest of lambs, much like the one Joshua had brought with him that night that Jesus was born.

"When we arrived, the courtyard was teeming with Herod's guard. Twelve there were, Joseph twelve of them. And the moment we entered the courtyard I saw one yelling into Leonard's face, 'Tell, old man! Where did the insurrectionist go with the child?'

"Leonard took a ragged breath—I could tell that they had already beaten him within an inch of his life—and looked defiantly into the eye of the captain of the guard. 'I will not tell!' he said. 'My life in place of his, Roman pig!'

"He had gone too far. The guard raised his hand
one last time and the club he had beaten the old inn
keeper with returned bloody. Leonard's body slumped
to the ground, his blood spilling into the fountain pool.

"That is when the captain of the guard saw us.
'You, shepherds,' he bellowed. 'Where can we find the
insurrectionist carpenter and his offspring?' We
answered truthfully that we did not know.

"The guards pushed passed us, and we rushed to
help Sarah tend to Leonard's body. We could not worry
about being unclean by contact with the body of our
fallen friend. All we could do was comfort his widow.
After we had helped her properly bury Leonard, Sarah
told us about your narrow escape, and that the guards
had shown up just hours after you had left with orders
to kill the child.

"The next week Herod's soldiers came through
killing all male children who were not yet two years old.
The cries of despair went up from all around
Bethlehem. In her bittersweet emotion at having lost
both Leonard and your family, but knowing that you
were safe, Sarah cried the loudest and the longest in the
ears of the public."

* * *

A year after our flight to Egypt, the angel
returned to my dreams.

"The ones who desire to see the child dead are

now gone. Take the child and his mother home to Israel," he told me.

We gathered our belongings and placed them on our donkey to start the long journey home. Passing through Palestine I learned that Herod's son Archelaus had taken the throne. My mind disturbed me. Could not this son of the one who killed an entire generation of boys not still be after Jesus? The angel returned to comfort me in my dreams that night.

"The child will be all right," he said. "Take your family to Galilee and set up your lodging, and all will go well with you."

And so, Mary and I took Jesus and returned to Nazareth.

Eleven

Life settled into a routine for us after we returned to Nazareth. Mary and I began our own family. No more angels visited in my dreams at night. The threat from the government disappeared. And Jesus grew.

He learned to show respect for his elders, remaining quiet until spoken to. I could almost swear that he sat listening, soaking in all the customs and traditions of our family, our town, our culture always curious but never intrusive. And Jesus grew.

He showed himself to be a better student than any apprentice I had ever worked with. When Jesus put his hand to the tools of my trade—the tools I had become one of the experts of the region with—they began to sing. The stools, chairs, tables, doors, benches he touched with the awl and chisel emerged as things of beauty. Many times requests came to me for work that I could not duplicate. Early as I worked with the lad, I saw his talent and allowed him to work alongside me. As a matter of fact, I recall a time or two that I sent Jesus out to the workbench without supervision, and the objects that he produced can be explained with nothing short of the description "miraculous."

When he played with his younger brother James and other children in the village, I watched the concern of a patient father ruffle his brow. From time to time I noticed that he would guide the younger children out of a particularly dubious activity that would surely have brought down the wrath of the local vegetable seller or cloth merchant. And Jesus grew.

Of an evening, I would sit at table with the lad and instruct him in much the way my father had instructed me on the days I could not make it to the synagogue school. On many days Jesus trekked to the synagogue to learn of our Lord God, of His ways, His purposes, His history with our people.

Jesus was interested in all walks of life. He watched the birds, the fish, the animals. He observed the rich and the poor, the religious and the reprobate, the old and the young. He studied the intricate as well as the simple. Everything and everyone he encountered basked in his undivided attention. Having Jesus around the house proved just another blessing on my life.

When Jesus turned twelve he inadvertently reminded me that God had only allowed Mary and I to raise him for a short while, then he must be about God's purpose. I remembered his miraculous birth, the escape from the hands of death, his wondrous life. I realized that he would soon take his life on a different course. The joy-giving flow of his mere presence would soon disappear from us.

* * *

Jesus' birthday marked the time we would take him with us to Jerusalem to celebrate the high holy days. He could finally join me in the men's court of the Temple. He would, of course, celebrate his bar mitzvah soon after this trip.

We traveled with many of the other families of our town. Others joined along our way to the Holy City. The trip marked a celebration in itself. I took the opportunity to gather Jesus' brothers and sisters close and teach them anew about the wandering of the children of Israel.

"Will we travel forty years to get to Jerusalem?" five-year-old James queried.

I laughed. "No, my son," I told him. "It will not even take one full year to arrive in Jerusalem. Nor will we be able to see and taste the wonder of manna, the heavenly bread that appeared each morning to sustain the lives of our forefathers. Though there are many families traveling with us, and you may play with many friends along the way, we had to bring enough food from home to sustain us on the journey to the Holy City and on our return.

"We are going to worship God and celebrate the festival, but we will not wander in search of the Promised Land—we are already there!"

The feasting and the celebration were like none other I had ever known. The fact that Jesus was at my side to participate in the worship and singing caused my voice to sing louder. And he sang with as much gusto as any other worshiper on hand. I remember being the proud father. After all, everyone claimed that I was his father; I had been his father; I could not think in any other terms.

Though we were tired, the trip home started as an extension of the celebration of the Lord God we had been a part of for the past several days. Our children, the older ones, found friends to play and argue with along the way. We continued to visit with friends we do not see except during these special trips to Jerusalem. It wasn't until we began to make camp for the night of the first day's journey home that we noticed that Jesus was not with us.

Mary and I began asking his friends if they had seen him. We visited other travelers' fires to see if perhaps they had invited him to take supper with them. As the minutes ticked away our pulses quickened, our anxiety grew, our fear multiplied. I ran from family to family. No one had seen him. Finally, Mary spoke.

"We must return," she said. "He may be hurt somewhere in the city."

We left the smaller children with our neighbor

with the promise to catch up to them as soon as we found Jesus. Then we returned to Jerusalem. We did not stop to rest that night and reached the outskirts of the city just as the gates were being opened at dawn.

"Have you seen our son?" I asked the gate keeper, and described Jesus to him.

"He has not come through here tonight," he replied.

I didn't wait to hear any more but led Mary by the hand as we rushed through the town retracing all our steps. We stopped at the marketplace, a veritable carnival for any young boy. He was not there. We stopped at the public house, a temptation to anyone who had never tasted spirits. He had not been seen. We stopped at relatives' houses, perhaps he had sought them out. No one remembered him after we had left. We stopped at Zechariah and Elizabeth's house; he and John had become fast friends. Zechariah said, "Maybe the Temple. He seemed quite interested in the study going on there."

Zechariah was right! Why had I not thought of that? I took Mary's arm and we literally ran to the Temple. And there was our son; there was Jesus.

Not only did he sit among the teachers of the law, but he seemed to be their teacher. He asked questions and he answered them. He spoke words of wisdom few have ever heard.

I did not hear them. I was overcome with relief, and then a wave of righteous indignation washed over me. Excusing myself to the scholars who encircled the

lad, I took him by the arm and led him out of the
Temple to where his mother waited. "What is the matter
with you, Jesus?" I scolded. "Your mother and I have
been worried sick."

With his clear, compassionate eyes he looked
upon us both and said, "Why?"

I was dumbfounded. *Why? Why?*

"Why would you worry?" he continued. "Didn't
you know I would be about my Father's work?"

His Father's work. My heart fell. He was right. I
was not his Father, and now I must let him go.

Twelve

We returned to Nazareth that day, and Jesus continued to grow. He grew strong, intelligent, witty. He grew in his ability to communicate with people. The skills I had seen in him as he brothered his siblings, brothers and sisters alike, grew prominent. The wisdom that I heard from his mouth as he questioned and answered the teachers of the law revealed itself even more after that day. He even amazed me working in the shop; how delicately he could shape a piece of wood until it no longer remained a piece of wood but an intricately designed, usable piece of furniture. I laughed when he presented the children of town with small wooden dolls he had fashioned from the scraps on the shop floor. Not only did the child's eyes come alive with excitement, but the doll Jesus had offered seemed to live in the hands of the expectant recipient. Jesus grew in his physical, mental and even his spiritual strength.

I proudly watched as he grew. I often put my arm around Mary's shoulder, and we would stand in the doorway and watch our brood. Then my eyes would light upon Jesus and my heart would soar. Looking Mary in the eye, I could see that she, too, continued to sing the melody placed in her heart the night the angel announced that she was to be the mother to the son of the Most High. This was a song that crescendoed at the stable the night angels proclaimed his birth to shepherds on a lonely Bethlehem hillside, a song that I could only grasp the edges of as the one chosen to guide his early years.

Zechariah is the priest. He is the one to ask about the things of God. I did ask one day and he replied obscurely, "Who knows the ways of God, my boy? We do not question; we accept and are blessed." He spoke from experience, I know, because the time the old priest questioned was a time filled with the struggle of inability to communicate. How difficult that time must have been. And still God's way triumphed.

Why does God do the things He does? Choose who He does? Work wonders for our eyes to behold? I do not know. I am just a simple carpenter.

What I do know is that God chose me for a special task, to be the husband of my beloved Mary and to provide a stable home for His son. I know that God took great effort in communicating to both Mary and me through His angels. He wanted us to know that, as unusual as the circumstances were, we had been exalted, lifted up, set apart. We were His servants, and He blessed us with a special task.

What would have happened if I had gone through with my plans to divorce Mary because of her obvious infidelity? I suspect that God would have found a way to provide the home structure for Jesus that He had intended through me. I would have been the only casualty.

Friend, let me advise you. Listen to the angels that speak to you. Follow the ways of God, even when they seem abnormal. God can give you so much more than you expect—even if you are just a simple carpenter like me.

Author's Note

Our knowledge of Joseph often makes him a difficult character to understand. The earthly father of Jesus, he made his living as a carpenter (see Matthew 13:55) which means that he made yokes for oxen, plows, and other tools. He also produced doors and latticework for homes as well as furniture and ladders.

Many carpenters would have become extremely skilled in the decorative art-working and etching that adorned the woodwork and some of the furniture. However, most of their work would have been hired by people who could afford only the bare essentials—a plain table with chairs or benches, utilitarian tools which required little or no fancy decoration.

The tools of the carpenter would have been crude examples of modern tools rough blades made from bronze or iron, and hammers made of wood.

The Scriptures hardly make mention of Joseph. In order to see into his character, we must read Matthew 1:19. The description here boils down to a word which can be translated in keeping with the character of God. Most translators use the word "just" or "righteous" to render this adjective. It indicates that, like his ancestor David, Joseph was a "man after God's own heart."

In this story I have attempted to show that righteousness in the love Joseph has for his wife Mary. I have also striven to remain true to the Scriptures. As in any fictional work, *Just a Simple Carpenter* takes great license in issues that are not part of the Scripture. At any point where the narrative might be faulty in its accuracy, the error lies with the limited knowledge of the author and not with the Author of Life who inspired the Holy Scriptures which I have tried to bring to life in this work.

I stopped the narrative at an obscure time which is some point after Jesus' encounter with the teachers in the Temple on the Passover of His twelfth year. This is the last mention we have of Joseph in the Bible. Traditionally, scholars have concluded that the carpenter probably died at some point not many years following this event. (See Luke 2:41-52 for the story of the young Jesus in the temple.)

For the fictional account of the innkeeper named Leonard and his shepherd friend, Jerome, read *Something Special at Leonard's Inn* published by Loom & Wheel in 1999.

About the Author

Benjamin Potter serves as pastor of a small east Texas Baptist church. He also teaches English at the local high school. When he is not preaching or teaching he loves to read and write fiction. He also enjoys camping, surfing the 'Net, and visiting with friends and family "live and in person."

Something Special at Leonard's Inn
A Tale of the First Christmas
by Benjamin Potter

Leonard is an old innkeeper trying to make ends meet when Caesar Augustus declares a census. Leonard and his wife expect to do very well, and reach a capacity crowd when two young people show up. The girl is pregnant. Leonard makes space for them in his stable and life will never be the same.

Jerome, one of the older shepherds of Bethlehem, remembers the days before the accident that shattered his friendship with Leonard. But nothing can keep him from seeing a miracle tonight—not even a twenty-year-old grudge.

——————————————————————————

Order your copy of Something Special at Leonard's Inn by sending $7.00, plus $2.00* shipping/handling to:

Loom & Wheel Publishing
P.O. Box 1691
Kildare, TX 75562

*For multiple copies send $7.00 for each book plus $2.00 for the first book and $.50 each for all other books

To order additional copies of **Something Special at Leonard's Inn** or **Just a Simple Carpenter**, complete the information below.

Ship to: (please print)
    Name _____
    Address _____
    City, State, Zip _____
    Day phone _____

_____ copies of *Something Special at Leonard's Inn*
                        @ $7.00 each $ _____
_____ copies of *Just a Simple Carpenter*   @ $10.00 each $ _____
                 Shipping/handling @ $2.00 $ _____
      ($.50 per book for second and following books)
                      Total amount $ _____

Make checks payable to **Loom & Wheel Publishing**
Send to: Loom & Wheel Publishing
P.O. Box 1691 • Kildare, TX 75562-1691

To order additional copies of **Something Special at Leonard's Inn** or **Just a Simple Carpenter**, complete the information below.

Ship to: (please print)
    Name _____
    Address _____
    City, State, Zip _____
    Day phone _____

_____ copies of *Something Special at Leonard's Inn*
                        @ $7.00 each $ _____
_____ copies of *Just a Simple Carpenter*   @ $10.00 each $ _____
            Postage and handling @ $2.00 per book $ _____
      ($.50 per book for second and following books)
                      Total amount $ _____

Make checks payable to **Loom & Wheel Publishing**
Send to: Loom & Wheel Publishing
P.O. Box 1691 • Kildare, TX 75562-1691